For Maria

Holiday House is registered in the U.S. Patent and Trademark Office
Printed and bound in March 2017 at Toppan Leefung, DongGuan City, China.
The art for this book was created with acrylic paint onto paper.
www.holidayhouse.com
First Edition
1 3 5 7 9 10 8 6 4 2
Library of Congress cataloging-in-publication data is available.

ISBN 978-0-8234-3753-5 (hardcover)

Rock-a-bye Baby

Jane Cabrera

Holiday House 🍎 New York

Rock-a-bye Baby,
on the treetop,
when the wind blows
the cradle will rock.

Rock-a-bye Squirrel,
high in the tree,
in Mommy's arms,
cozy as can be.

Rock-a-bye Robin,
in a nook in the tree,
tucked in your nest,
as snug as can be.

Rock-a-bye Caterpillar,
hung from the tree,
gently swaying,
cocooned as can be.

Rock-a-bye Owlet,
in the trunk of the tree,
in your hidey-hole,
as safe as can be.

Rock-a-bye Spider,
spun round the tree,
in your delicate web,
as sparkly as can be.

Rock-a-bye Bat,
deep in the tree,
nestled upside down,
as dark as can be.

Rock-a-bye Snake,
on a branch of the tree,
coiled round and round,
as tight as can be.

Rock-a-bye Mouse,
under roots of the tree,
rocked to and fro,
as quiet as can be.

Rock-a-bye Fawn,
in the shade of the tree,
in sweet-scented flowers,
as soft as can be.

Rock-a-bye Bunny,
burrowed under the tree,
all hidden away,
as warm as can be.

Rock-a-bye Baby,
WHAT A BEAUTIFUL TREE!
Sleep now, my darling,
HAPPY as can be.

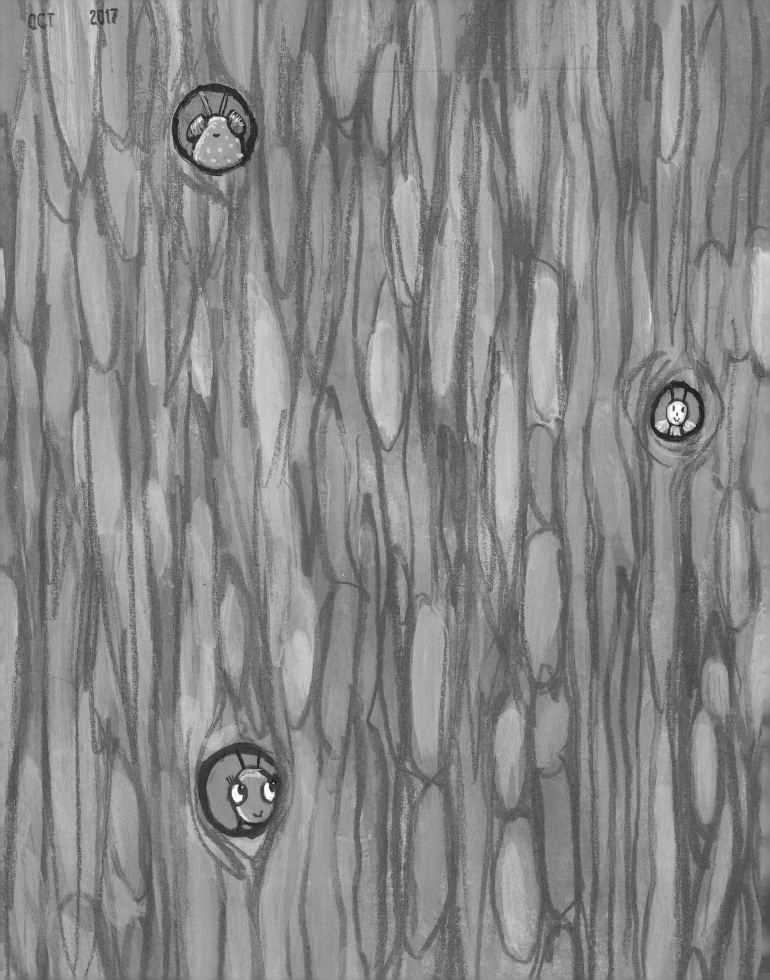